Also by Serge Bloch (with Davide Cali)

The Enemy

First English-language edition published in
Australia and New Zealand in 2011 by
Wilkins Farago Pty Ltd (ABN 14 081 592 770)
PO Box 78, Albert Park, Victoria 3206, Australia

Orignally published in French as *Sam et son papa* © Bayard Éditions 2009

Teachers' notes & other material: www.wilkinsfarago.com.au

National Library of Australia Cataloguing-in-Publication entry
Author: Bloch, Serge.
Title: Sam and his dad / Serge Bloch.
ISBN: 9780980607086 (hbk.)
Target Audience: For primary school age.
Subjects: Family life–Juvenile fiction.
Dewey Number: A823.4

Printed in China by Everbest Printing
Distributed by The Scribo Group (Australia) and
Addenda (New Zealand)

serge bloch

Sam and his dad

WILKINS_farago_

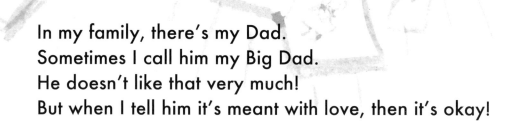

In my family, there's my Dad.
Sometimes I call him my Big Dad.
He doesn't like that very much!
But when I tell him it's meant with love, then it's okay!

In my family, there's also my little brother. His name's Leon.
He's always ready to muck around with me ...

... even if he sometimes wrecks my buildings.

In my family, there's also my Mum.
My-darling-Mummy-whom-I-love-to-bits.
She makes me a bottle even though I'm a bit too big for them.

Then there's me ...
My name is Sam, which is short for Samuel.

But I prefer Supersam!

Dad knows how to make all kinds of
dress-up costumes. I ask him to turn me
into a monster or an enormous animal
and TA-DA! I'm transformed.

Dad knows how to draw too.
'Draw me a wolf with great big teeth,' I ask.

'And then draw me a bird, a pigeon,
and also the sea with a lighthouse, crabs and fish.'

His job is drawing.

In the street with Dad, I jump in all the puddles,

I climb on all the posts ...

... I'm a little monkey!

When I go to school, Dad is always in a hurry.
He says, 'Hurry up, Samuel, we're going to be late!'

But when Dad is lagging behind me, he says,
'Hey, wait up, mate!'

If we cut through the park, I immediately start chasing the pigeons.

One day, I'm going to catch one, put salt on its tail feathers and cook it!
Well, maybe.

When we head to the country, my Dad drives.
I say to him, 'Don't drive too fast, the wheels will fall off!'

In the car, we play, eat sweets and then everyone sleeps.
Except Dad!

When we finally arrive at our house, no-one wants to sleep, of course. Except Dad!

We go for walks, often to Mr Roy's farm.

Sometimes we go by foot.

Sometimes by bike.

There are cows at Mr. Roy's farm ... and cow poo!

And roosters, hens, rabbits ...

... and a dog, who isn't very friendly!

I love animals.
But I'm also wary of them.

I have hens, roosters, bulls –
big ones, little ones, but no real ones.

I have loads of them in a suitcase.
I have more animals than Noah's Ark,
which was a very big boat full of animals.

I make farms and zoos and even big processions of animals.

Often, I have a little play fight with Dad
when he is not working.
They're great fun.

I always win!

We also play the wolf and the little pig.
I pretend to be very frightened in my little house ...

... but because it's made of brick, Dad can't get in!

Afterwards, we pretend to be hunters, and the wolves hide because they're so scared of us.

I'm very good at gymnastics.

Gymnastics includes somersaults, balancing
and all sorts of acrobatics.

When Dad holds me up to the ceiling,
I laugh and scream very loudly so Mum comes.
She's always terrified!

I love stories.
Quick stories when we're in a hurry in the morning.
Stories at dinner to make me eat my food.
Above all, I love the story about the giant who traps a dragon
and puts him in the stew!

I also like the stories Grandma
records for me.

I listen to them all day.
But sometimes Dad has had enough.
He gets angry and tells me to turn Grandma off.

In the evening, Mum reads us stories –
really long stories to keep the light on as long as possible.

I like stories with monsters
in them the best.
Afterwards, I get nightmares ...

... and I go into my parents' bed.
Sometimes, the spot is already taken.

But there's usually a little space
for me to squeeze into!